This igloo book belongs to:

..............................................

**igloobooks**

Published in 2013
by Igloo Books Ltd
Cottage Farm
Sywell
NN6 0BJ
www.igloobooks.com

FIR003 0513
2 4 6 8 10 9 7 5 3 1
ISBN 978-1-78197-474-2

Written by Xanna Eve Chown
Illustrated by Annabelle Spenceley

Printed and manufactured in China

# You're My
# Best Friend

igloobooks

You're my best friend in the whole world. We have so much fun together and you always know the best games to play.

We race to the swings in the playground and take it in turns to push.
Whoosh! We swing so high it feels like flying.

When we have a tea party with all our teddies and Dolly, too,
you always let me have the best spotty teacup.

You pour the teddies their tea and I ask them if they want
more cake. We giggle as we lick the icing off the top.

You're my best friend because if I fall over and bump my
knee, you come running to give me a hug.

You tell me to cheer up and your hug makes me feel
so much better, I forget that I was upset.

We tell each other everything and when I whisper my biggest secrets, I know you'll keep them.

You trust me with your secrets, too, like the time we dressed
up in your mummy's clothes and got them all muddy.

You're my best friend because you never forget my birthday. You always come to my party and sing, "Happy Birthday" louder than anyone.

You gave me a special necklace that looks just like yours.
When we hold them together, they make the shape of a heart.

You come to visit me when I'm feeling ill and tell me funny stories about what happened at school that day.

You make me cards that say, "Get well soon!"
and paint them with pretty fairies, princesses and flowers.

You're my best friend because we like the same things
most of the time, but when we don't, it doesn't matter.

When we make yummy ice cream sundaes, you like strawberry ice cream, but I always choose chocolate.

You always make sleepovers so much fun.
We make a tent with our blankets, then sit inside and tell stories.

When we hear noises in the dark, you say, "Don't worry!"
and shine a torch to show me that it's just the cat.

You're my best friend because I miss you when we're far apart and can't wait to see you when you come back.

You always send me postcards from your holidays,
with little seashells and sand stuck to the bottom.

Most of all, you're my best friend because you're you!
There's no one else like you in the whole world.

I never, ever feel lost, or sad, or lonely when you're around,
because you make everything better.

You're my best friend and I know we'll be friends forever.